Note to parents, carers and teachers

Read it yourself is a series of modern stories, favourite characters and traditional tales written in a simple way for children who are learning to read. The books can be read independently or as part of a guided reading session.

Each book is carefully structured to include many high-frequency words vital for first reading. The sentences on each page are supported closely by pictures to help with understanding, and to offer lively details to talk about.

The books are graded into four levels that progressively introduce wider vocabulary and longer stories as a reader's ability and confidence grows.

Ideas for use

- Begin by looking through the book and talking about the pictures. Has your child heard this story before?

- Help your child with any words he does not know, either by helping him to sound them out or supplying them yourself.

- Developing readers can be concentrating so hard on the words that they sometimes don't fully grasp the meaning of what they're reading. Answering the puzzle questions on pages 30 and 31 will help with understanding.

For more information and advice on Read it yourself and book banding, visit **www.ladybird.com/readityourself**

Book Band 5

Level 2 is ideal for children who have received some reading instruction and can read short, simple sentences with help.

Special features:

Frequent repetition of main story words and phrases

Short, simple sentences

Large, clear type

Careful match between story and pictures

One day, a nut fell on Chicken Licken. "Ouch! The sky is falling down!" said Chicken Licken. "I must tell the king."

6

7

On the way, they met Ducky Lucky.

"The sky is falling down," said Chicken Licken. "I'm going to tell the king."

17

16

Educational Consultant: Geraldine Taylor
Book Banding Consultant: Kate Ruttle

A catalogue record for this book is available from the British Library

Published by Ladybird Books Ltd
80 Strand, London, WC2R 0RL
A Penguin Company

003

© LADYBIRD BOOKS LTD MMX. This edition MMXIII
Ladybird, Read It Yourself and the Ladybird Logo are registered or
unregistered trademarks of Ladybird Books Limited.

ISBN: 978-0-72327-296-0

Printed in China

Chicken Licken

Illustrated by Richard Johnson

One day, a nut fell on Chicken Licken.

"Ouch! The sky is falling down!" said Chicken Licken. "I must tell the king."

On the way, he met
Henny Penny.

"The sky is falling down,"
said Chicken Licken.
"I'm going to tell the king."

9

"I'll come too,"
said Henny Penny.

And off they went
to find the king.

On the way, they met
Cocky Locky.

"The sky is falling down,"
said Chicken Licken.
"I'm going to tell
the king."

"I'll come too,"
said Cocky Locky.

And off they went
to find the king.

To the Castle

On the way, they met
Ducky Lucky.

"The sky is falling down,"
said Chicken Licken.
"I'm going to tell the king."

"I'll come too,"
said Ducky Lucky.

And off they went
to find the king.

To the Castle

On the way, they met
Drakey Lakey.

"The sky is falling down,"
said Chicken Licken.
"I'm going to tell the king."

"I'll come too,"
said Drakey Lakey.

And off they went
to find the king.

To the Farm   To the Castle

23

On the way, they met
Goosey Loosey.

"The sky is falling down,"
said Chicken Licken.
"I'm going to tell the king."

"I'll come too," said
Goosey Loosey.

And off they went
to find the king.

On the way, they met
Foxy Loxy.

"The sky is falling down,"
they said. "We're going
to tell the king."

"The king lives here,"
said Foxy Loxy.
"Follow me."

And that was the end of Chicken Licken, Henny Penny, Cocky Locky, Ducky Lucky, Drakey Lakey and Goosey Loosey!

How much do you remember about the story of Chicken Licken? Answer these questions and find out!

- What falls on Chicken Licken's head?

- What does he think is happening?

- Who does Chicken Licken go to tell?

- Where does Foxy Loxy take everyone?

Look at the pictures and match them to the story words.

Chicken Licken

Henny Penny

Ducky Lucky

Goosey Loosey

Foxy Loxy

Read it yourself with Ladybird

Tick the books you've read!

For beginner readers who can read short, simple sentences with help.

Level 2

- Beauty and the Beast ☐
- Chicken Licken ☐
- Little Red Riding Hood ☐
- Nature Trail ☐
- Sports Day ☐
- Pirate School ☐
- Rumpelstiltskin ☐
- Sleeping Beauty ☐
- The Gingerbread Man ☐
- Sly Fox and Red Hen ☐
- The Tale of Jemima Puddle-Duck ☐
- The Three Little Pigs ☐
- Why Lion Roarrrs! ☐
- The Big Race ☐
- Town Mouse and Country Mouse ☐
- Dom's Dragon ☐

For more confident readers who can read simple stories with help.

Level 3

- You won't like this present as much as I DO! ☐
- The Elves and the Shoemaker ☐
- Hansel and Gretel ☐
- Harry and the Bucketful of Dinosaurs ☐
- Jack and the Beanstalk ☐
- Furi on Music Island ☐
- Poppet Stows Away ☐
- Rapunzel ☐
- The Red Knight ☐